THE GOBLIN HAT
AND OTHER STORIES

The
Goblin Hat

and
Other Stories

by
ENID BLYTON

Illustrated by
Dorothy Hamilton

AWARD PUBLICATIONS

For further information on Enid Blyton please visit *www.blyton.com*

ISBN 978-1-84135-439-2

Illustrations copyright © Award Publications Limited

First published 1954 as *Enid Blyton's Friendly Story Book*
by Brockhampton Press Limited

First published by Award Publications Limited 1987
This edition first published 2005

Published by Award Publications Limited,
The Old Riding School, The Welbeck Estate,
Worksop, Nottinghamshire, S80 3LR

12 5

Printed in the United Kingdom

CONTENTS

1

The Forgotten Canary

There was once a little canary called Feathers. He lived in a blue cage in Katie's nursery, and he belonged to Katie.

At first Katie loved Feathers and looked after him well. Each day she cleaned his cage, gave him new seed and fresh water. At teatime she gave him a lump of sugar, and every day she looked for a bit of groundsel to give him for a treat.

Then, when it was no longer fun to look after him, Katie began to get tired of him. She gave him no groundsel. She forgot his lump of sugar.

One day she didn't clean his cage. Another day she didn't give him any fresh seed, because she thought he had enough. She didn't guess how he looked forward to turning over fresh seed every morning.

And then, worst of all, she forgot his water. Mother saw that he had very little water, and scolded Katie, and the little girl was ashamed. For four days she cleaned his cage properly, gave him food and water, and even picked a bit of groundsel for him, and put in a dish of water for a bath.

Then she forgot again. Feathers was very unhappy. He could not sing because he was so thirsty. Twenty times a day he went to his water-dish and looked at it with his head on one side, hoping and hoping that there might be just a drop of water there – but of course there wasn't.

'Tweet, tweet!' called Feathers loudly. Katie was putting her dolls to bed and took no notice. 'TWEET, TWEET!' called Feathers again. It wasn't a bit of good.

'I'm in this little cage and I can't get out to find food and water for myself,' thought the canary sadly. 'If I were a sparrow I could hunt for seed for myself. If I were a chaffinch I could go to the nearest pool for a drink. But I'm a canary in a cage, and I can't look after myself at all.'

9

Poor little canary! He had no drink for two days, and the seed in his little dish was nothing but husks. It was dreadful! He drooped his little yellow head and thought he would die.

'Have you fed the canary this morning?' said Mother, putting her head in at the door.

Katie knew she hadn't – and she knew that Mother would be very angry with her if she found out that her canary had no food. So what did the naughty little girl say, 'Oh, yes, Mother, Feathers is quite all right!'

It was a naughty story, and Katie was ashamed of herself for telling it, and went very red. But Mother didn't see her red face. She was busy and went off to do some ironing.

'I can give Feathers some food and water at once,' Katie said to herself. 'Then it won't be a story.'

But it *was* a story, wasn't it? And do you know, just as Katie was going to take down the cage to clean it, Mother called her. 'Katie! I want you to go and

get some cakes for me. Hurry now, because there isn't much time.'

'I'll do the canary afterwards,' thought Katie, and ran off. She didn't remember to do the canary when she came back, though Feathers was hoping and hoping that she would.

The next morning, very early, a little brown sparrow looked in at the nursery window. He sometimes came to have a word with Feathers. He chirruped to him.

'Chirrup! Chirrup! How are you, Feathers?'

11

'Not at all well,' said poor Feathers sadly. 'I've had no food and no water for a long time. I think I shall soon die.'

'I'll bring you something to eat,' said the sparrow. He flew off and came back with a few seeds in his beak. He sat on the cage-wire and dropped them through to Feathers.

'I can't bring you water,' he said; 'I don't know how to. But, Feathers, I'm going to tell the little pixie who lives in the rockery. She may be able to help you.'

So he flew off to tell Chinks the pixie. Chinks was angry, and sorry to hear about poor Feathers.

'I won't let that horrid Katie have a canary!' she said. 'I won't, I won't! I'll rescue Feathers myself and set him free.'

'But Chinks, if you do that, everyone will see him flying about, and he'll be caught again,' said the sparrow. 'You know what a bright yellow he is. If only he were a common brown like us, he'd never be noticed.'

'Don't bother me for a moment,' said Chinks. 'I want to think.' So she thought hard, whilst the sparrow sat by in silence.

'I believe there is a pot of brown paint in the gardener's shed,' said Chinks at

13

last, getting up. 'I'll rescue Feathers, paint him brown, and let him live with you sparrows. You can teach him how to find seeds, can't you?'

'Certainly,' said the sparrow, pleased. 'May I come with you and see what you do, Chinks?'

He went with Chinks. The pixie flew in at the nursery window. Katie was having her breakfast downstairs with her mother. There was no one in the nursery.

Chinks set down the brown paint on

the window-sill and flew to the cage.
'Feathers! Are you well enough to fly out
of the window if I open your cage door
and set you free?' she asked.

'I think so,' said the poor canary, who
felt very weak indeed. 'I'll try. But what
will Katie say when she finds my cage
empty? Hadn't we better leave a note for
her to say that I've gone?'

'Yes,' said Chinks. 'We *will* leave a
note – and I will write it!'

She went to where Katie kept her
writing things and tore off a sheet of
paper. She took a pencil and wrote. This
is what Chinks said:

Dear Katie,
I have gone away
because you don't
give me food or
water and I am
nearly dead. You
are a horrid, unkind
girl. Tweets from
Feathers.

15

Chinks opened the door of the cage and Feathers flew out. He managed to get to the window-sill, and there he perched, feeling rather wobbly. Chinks put the note at the bottom of the cage, and then shut the cage door again. She flew to the window-sill and picked up the pot of paint.

'Just come with me to the holly tree,' she said. 'It isn't bare like the other trees, and you can hide there whilst I paint you brown. Then you'll be like the sparrows.'

They went to the holly tree, and in the shade of its prickly leaves Chinks painted Feathers a plain brown colour. She even painted a little black bib under his chin, just like the father sparrows were wearing then, and little bars of white in his wing feathers.

When he was finished he sat in the sun to dry. He looked like a sparrow, except his legs were a pinker colour and not quite so thick as a sparrow's.

The sparrows came round him and made him welcome. 'Come and we'll

The Forgotten Canary

show you where the best seeds are to be found,' they chirruped. 'You shall be one of us!'

So Feathers went with them, and soon became very clever at finding food and water. How lovely it was to drink from puddles, and to peck at wild bits of groundsel whenever he found them!

And what about Katie? Well, after breakfast she came into the nursery, and remembered her canary. 'Oh dear!' she said. 'I meant to have cleaned the cage yesterday and I forgot again. What a nuisance! I really must do it today.'

So she took down the cage, but to her enormous surprise Feathers wasn't there! She looked and she looked, but Feathers simply wasn't there at all.

She ran to the door and called her

mother. 'Mother! Mother! Have you let
Feathers out?'

'Of course not,' said Mother, running
up. 'He must be there! The door of the
cage is shut.'

But the canary was certainly gone.
Mother spied the little note in the
bottom of the cage. She opened the door,
put in her hand, and picked up the note.
She read it:

Dear Katie,
I have gone away because you don't give me food or water, and I am nearly dead. You are a horrid, unkind girl.

Tweets from
Feathers.

Mother put down the note and looked at Katie, who had gone very red.

'Katie! What a dreadful thing! So that's why your canary has gone. Well, it serves you right. If you can't look after something in your care, you have no right to keep it. I'm ashamed of you.'

Katie burst into tears. She remembered how sweetly Feathers had sung. She remembered how he put his little yellow head on one side when she spoke to him. She remembered how prettily he splashed in his bath. Now he was gone and would never come back.

'It serves you right,' said Mother. 'I only hope poor little Feathers will be able to feed himself out in the garden.'

She needn't have worried. Feathers is

quite all right with the sparrows. The only thing is – he got caught in the rain the other day, and some of the brown paint came off, showing his yellow colour underneath. So if you see a sparrow with patches of yellow, you'll know who it is – it's Feathers!

2

Pockets in his Knees

'Hey!' cried Chinky, the elf, to a bee flying by. 'Give me a lift, will you?'

'Where to?' said the honey bee, slowing down a little, his strong wings fanning the air and making quite a draught.

'I've got to take these parcels to Old Man Kindly,' said Chinky. 'Very important. He wants them for a spell today.'

'What's in the parcels?' said the bee, flying down beside Chinky. 'Are they heavy?'

'No. Small and light,' said Chinky. 'Keep your feelers out of them now! We mustn't even *look* inside!'

'All right. I'll take you,' said the bee. 'Hop on my back. But for goodness sake

hold tight, because the last time I gave someone a lift – let me see, who was it now? Oh, yes, it was Bobo – he fell off, and as he fell a swallow snapped him up, thinking he was an extra large fly. Dreadful shock for him. He only just got away in time.'

'I'll certainly hold tight,' said Chinky, and he climbed on to the bee's brown back. He took his parcels with him, but it was very difficult to hold them and to hold tightly to the bee's back, too.

'Wait, wait!' cried Chinky in panic, as the bee's wings began to whirr. 'I'm not ready. I can't hold on with both hands because of Old Man Kindly's parcels.'

The bee stopped whirring his wings. 'Put the parcels in a bag and sling the bag over your shoulder,' he said sensibly.

'Haven't got a bag,' said Chinky. 'Bother! I've dropped one of the parcels. Now I'll have to get off and pick it up.'

'We shall never be off!' said the bee impatiently. 'Put the parcels in your pockets, Chinky.'

'I haven't any pockets either,' said Chinky. 'What about you, Bee? Haven't *you* any pockets?'

'Yes. But they are full already,' said the bee.

'Full! What of? And where *are* your pockets?' asked Chinky in surprise.

'In my knees,' said the bee. 'Didn't you know that bees have nice little pockets there?'

'No, I didn't,' said Chinky, peering over the bee's body to look. 'Yes, I can see them! What a funny place to have pockets! And whatever have you got in them? They're full of yellow stuff.'

'Yes. I've been collecting pollen to take back to the hive, to make pollen-bread,' said the bee. 'I stuff it into my knee-pockets. I was just going back to the hive when you called me.'

'I say, Bee – I suppose you wouldn't empty your pockets and let me put my parcels in them, would you?' said Chinky. 'Then I could have my hands

25

free, and my parcels would be quite safe. I could hold on tightly.'

'All right,' said the bee, and he emptied all the yellow pollen from his pockets. 'Now – put your parcels in, but do be quick.'

Chinky stuffed his tiny parcels into the bee's pockets, then held on tightly as the bee rose into the air with a loud humming of wings. He flew with him to Old Man Kindly's cottage set in the midst of the moorland. 'Wait for me, and take me back, Bee,' cried Chinky, and he disappeared into the cottage.

Old Man Kindly was delighted to see him and the parcels of magic for his new spell. 'This is really very kind of you,' he said. 'Now what will you have as a reward for your kindness, Chinky?'

'Well, *I* don't want a reward,' said Chinky, 'but you could perhaps reward the bee who brought me and my parcels here, Old Man Kindly. He let me stuff my parcels into his knee pockets, so that I could have both hands free to hold on with.'

26

Pockets in his Knees

Old Man Kindly went out to the waiting bee. 'I hear you have been helpful and kind,' he said. 'Look around you at my moorland. The heather is out and full of honey. Help yourself, bee, and take as much as you like!'

'Heather honey!' buzzed the bee joyfully. 'Best in the world! Thank you very much indeed.'

And off he went to feast and to take back to his hive as much as he could carry. Chinky went with him, enjoying licks of honey *and* a lovely ride.

'Thanks for lending me your knee-pockets!' he said to the bee. 'I never knew you had any before!'

Did *you* know that a bee had pockets in his knees? You didn't? Well, watch the bees coming and going to the flowers in your garden, and you'll soon see how they pack the yellow pollen into their pockets. Isn't it a clever idea?

3

One Thing Leads to Another

It was the baby doll's birthday. She was one year old. Janet made a fuss of her because it was her birthday, and she gave her a lovely present.

'There you are, Rosebud,' she said to her doll, and she pinned something to her bib. 'There's a beautiful brooch for you. It came out of my nicest Christmas cracker, and I saved it for your birthday.'

Rosebud was very proud and pleased. She showed her brooch to the toys that night. 'I'm sure it must be real gold,' she said. 'And look at the bright blue stone in the middle – isn't it lovely?'

'Can I try it on?' asked the fat little teddy bear. He was a funny little thing, dressed in a red jersey and blue trousers.

He was proud of the trousers because they had real pockets, and he was always putting his hands in them.

'No, you can't try it on,' said the doll. 'You would break it. You're clumsy.'

'You'd better keep it safe somewhere,' said the golliwog. 'It's valuable, you know, Rosebud. You wouldn't want anyone to steal it, would you?'

'Oh, dear, no,' said Rosebud. 'It's very, very precious. Where shall I keep it?'

The toys thought hard. Then the pink cat said she knew of a good place.

'What about inside the dolls' house?' she said. 'In the drawer of the chest of drawers upstairs in the little bedroom. It would be quite safe there.'

The biggest of the dolls' house dolls said she would put it there, and she ran up the stairs of the little house with the

beautiful brooch. She shut it carefully into the drawer.

Now, one night, after the toys had played together, and then gone to sleep tired out, the teddy bear couldn't go to sleep at all. He lay in the toy cupboard and tossed and turned. Then he got up and walked out.

'Perhaps a walk round the nursery will do me good,' he thought. So he set off round the room – and very soon he came to the dolls' house. It was dark and quiet because everyone in it was asleep.

The teddy bear was tall enough to look in at the bedroom windows. He pressed his nose against the glass and looked in at the bedroom where the beautiful brooch had been put. He could see the chest of drawers very dimly.

A naughty thought came into his mind. Suppose he opened the window, put his arm inside and pulled open the little drawer - he could get the brooch!

'I'd only just try it on to see how I looked, and then I'd put it back,'

thought the bear. 'Nobody would ever know, and no harm would be done.'

So he opened the window very quietly, put in his fat little arm, and pulled open the drawer of the tiny wooden chest. He felt about - and there was the brooch!

He took it out and looked at it.

'How beautiful!' he said. 'I'll just pin it on myself, see how I look, walk around the nursery once with it on and then put it back.'

He tried to pin it on to the front of his jersey, but he pushed too hard, and – oh dear me, the pin broke right off!

The bear stared at the broken brooch in horror. It was no use now. The pin had broken off. It couldn't be pinned to anyone again. How simply dreadful!

What was he to do? Should he put the broken brooch back and say nothing about it? Or should he keep it and try to mend it?

He heard a stirring in the dolls' house. Oh dear – he couldn't put it back then! Someone would hear him. He slipped the broken brooch and pin into his pocket and went quietly off to the toy cupboard. He was very worried.

He fell asleep at last – and in the morning what a to-do! Rosebud had asked for her brooch and it wasn't in the drawer. Who had taken it?

Rosebud cried bitterly. 'I did so love it,' she sobbed. 'Who's been so unkind as to take it? Why did they steal it?'

'I expect someone wanted to wear it at a party,' said the teddy bear feeling very guilty indeed, but not brave enough to own up.

'Oh, yes – the mice are having a party down in their hole tonight!' said the golliwog. 'I wonder if it was one of them who stole it last night. What do you think, Teddy?'

'Yes, I expect one of them did,' said the bear, feeling dreadful.

'Then that's the last time we allow the mice to come and play with us,' said the pink cat firmly. 'I shall tell the kitchen cat to come up here each night and scare the mice.'

The bear felt even more miserable. He had a great friend among the mouse family, a little mouse called Whiskery. Now Whiskery would be too afraid to come and see him again.

'One thing leads to another,' thought the bear mournfully. 'First I do a naughty thing and borrow the brooch when I shouldn't. Then I break it. Then I say maybe somebody has taken it to wear at a party. Then the golliwog remembers there's a mouse-party, and thinks the mice took it – and now the cat's to come up each night and scare them away – so that maybe I'll never, never see dear little Whiskery again!'

The pink cat was as good as her word. She asked the kitchen cat to come up and watch for the mice, and the big tabby said yes, of course she would. She was always ready to watch for mice.

Now, the mice wouldn't have come up that night because they were having their party – but it happened that little Whiskery wanted to go to the nursery and give her friend, the teddy bear, a bit of the lovely party cake. So up she skipped, and popped out of her hole.

'Teddy!' she squeaked. 'Teddy, I've got something for you!'

The kitchen cat was there. She pounced – and there was poor Whiskery under her big paw! How she squealed!

The bear was horrified. What! His friend Whiskery was caught! And all because of something *he* had done! Oh no, no, he couldn't let little Whiskery be caught and eaten!

He rushed at the big cat and tried to push her paw away. 'Let Whiskery go, she's my friend,' he cried. He gave the cat's paw such a big shove that he moved it - and Whiskery shot out, limping, because one of her legs had been hurt. She raced down her hole.

The cat was angry. She hit the bear hard with her paw and sent him rolling over and over on the floor. And, oh dear, the pin that was in his pocket ran right into him and pricked him terribly. He lay groaning on the floor.

The toys ran to help him up. 'Brave Teddy! You saved Whiskery's life!' they cried. 'What's hurting you? Why are you groaning?'

'Something is sticking into me,' sobbed the bear. 'Just *here*!'

The golliwog put his hand into the bear's pocket and felt about. 'There's a

pin here, or something,' he said. *'That's* what's sticking into you!'

How *everyone* stared! Why, here was the stolen brooch belonging to Rosebud – and it was broken. How did it come to be in the bear's pocket?

The bear went red from head to foot with shame, and he really looked most peculiar. He hung his head.

'I took it last night just to try it on,' he said. 'Not to steal. Only to try. And I broke the pin. I thought I could mend it. Then everyone thought it was stolen – and – and . . .'

'*You* said someone might have taken it to wear at a party and I remembered the mouse-party – and we were angry and got the kitchen cat up here – and your friend Whiskery nearly got killed,' said the golliwog in an awful voice.

'I know. I can't tell you how sorry I am,' said the bear, still hanging his head. 'I'll pack my things and go. You won't want me here any more. I'm so ashamed. It only seemed a little thing to do, to borrow the brooch for a minute.'

'Little tiny wrong things lead to much *bigger* wrong things!' said the golliwog, still in a dreadfully stern voice. 'Once you begin going wrong you never know where it will end.'

'I know,' wept the bear. 'I've done wrong - and you can't think what a shock I had when I saw poor Whiskery being caught. I feel quite ill when I remember it. I'll go and pack my bag now - but please don't think too unkindly of me when I've gone.'

He went off to pack his little bag. He

was very unhappy. The toys talked together in low voices.

They were shocked and sorry and upset. How *could* the bear do such a thing?

He soon came out with his little bag marked T.B. 'Good-bye,' he said. 'Please do forgive me, won't you?'

Rosebud called to him. 'Teddy, we don't want you to go. You're sorry for what you did, and you'll never do such a thing again. The golliwog has mended my brooch. Whiskery isn't badly hurt.

The kitchen cat has promised to stay down in the kitchen, now we know it wasn't the mice who took the brooch. So everything has been put right.'

'Don't you *really* want me to go?' said the bear, beaming happily.

'No. We all want you to stay,' said the golliwog. 'But just remember, Teddy – one thing leads to another, SO BE CAREFUL!'

It's quite true, isn't it – one thing does lead to another, and sometimes a tiny thing becomes a much bigger one. I'm going to be careful, too!

4

The Goblin Hat

There was once a very mischievous goblin who had a magic hat. It was a very big one, with a wide, curly brim, and it was bright red except for its feather, which was blue.

It was a very magical hat. When the goblin put it on he couldn't be seen! It made him invisible at once.

But, of course, the hat could be seen, so it was a strange sight to see the hat bobbing along the street, its blue feather waving, and nobody underneath it! It made people feel very frightened indeed.

When the old Balloon-Woman saw the hat coming along by itself, she gave a scream and ran away, leaving all her colourful balloons tied to the back of her chair. There weren't many of them

left when at last she ventured back! The goblin had taken most of them, and was a mile away, with only his hat and the balloons to be seen!

And when he walked into Mr. Buns' cake shop, the big hat bobbing on top of his invisible head and his footsteps going click-clack on the floor, Mr. Buns fled to the room at the back of his shop at once.

'There must be something wrong with my eyes!' he thought. 'And my ears, too. I heard footsteps from feet I couldn't see, and saw a hat worn by somebody who wasn't there!'

Well, it didn't take long for the mischievous goblin to help himself to a big jam sandwich, a chocolate cake and a dozen jammy buns. Out he went, delighted, and everyone he met ran away in fright to see a big hat, a jam sandwich, a chocolate cake and a dozen buns bobbing along down the street. Even the butcher's fierce dog ran away, though he would dearly have liked to snap at the buns.

Now, Mr. Plod the policeman was puzzled to hear these odd stories, but he soon got to the bottom of the mystery. 'It's the Tiresome Goblin,' he said. 'He's got a big hat to wear that makes him invisible. Next time you see that hat, catch the invisible body below it; whip off the hat, and you'll see you've got old Tiresome! Then bring him to me.'

Well, after that everyone waited for the hat to appear. But Tiresome the goblin heard about this, and he was frightened. He wasn't going to be caught! No, he knew what that would mean – spankings and bread and water, and being locked up for weeks.

So what do you think he did? He went and caught Farmer Meadow's biggest billy-goat, and he tied the magic hat to Billy's horns!

Well, of course, Billy vanished as soon as the hat was on his horns! He was there all right, but he couldn't be seen. Tiresome, the goblin, chuckled to himself and gave Billy a shove. 'Now, you go walking down the village street,

looking as grand as can be in my hat –
and don't you stand any nonsense from
anyone!' he said.

So off went the billy-goat, stepping
proudly, not knowing that not a scrap of
him could be seen except the hat. Down
the village street he went and everyone
yelled in excitement.

'Here's Tiresome the Goblin! There's
his hat, so he must be under it, though
we can't see him. Catch him, catch him!'

'Leave this to me,' said Mr. Stamp-
About, who was always ready to show

how clever he was. 'I'll manage him!'

He flung himself at the goat, thinking it was just a goblin he was getting hold of. Billy was most surprised. He put down his head and butted Mr. Stamp-About so hard that he rolled into the gutter.

Mr. Stamp-About was in a fine old temper when he got up. He rolled up his sleeves and rushed up to the hat, which was all he could see. The hat was bobbing about like anything, because the goat was prancing madly, ready to butt Mr. Stamp-About again.

Mr. Stamp-About made a grab at the hat, knowing that if he could get it off, the person wearing it could easily be seen. But the hat was firmly tied to Billy's horns and wouldn't come off.

Poor Mr. Stamp-About found himself butted and biffed unmercifully, and although he tried to clutch at Billy here and there, Billy always got away.

'This goblin's hairy!' he cried. 'And my word, he's got a tail. Think of that! I felt it distinctly. I felt his beard, too.'

The Goblin Hat

Well, billy-goats always wear beards and tails, so that wasn't surprising. Mr. Stamp-About hadn't time to say any more because Billy butted him so hard that he flew into the air and landed in the middle of a case of Mr. Apple's best tomatoes. After that Mr. Stamp-About didn't want to have anything more to do with the hat.

Billy went quite mad. He rushed at this person and that, butting and biffing happily. People went down like ninepins – and dear me, when Mr. Plod the policeman came up, most surprised to see people tumbling about, Billy ran at him, too!

Over he went, his helmet knocked down on his nose. 'What's all this?' he began. 'Oh – it's Tiresome the Goblin, is it, behaving like this! That's his hat!'

Well, nobody could do anything with Billy the goat, and nobody could get the hat. People were beginning to get frightened, when somebody else came up the street. It was Tiresome the Goblin, though nobody knew it! They had never seen him before, because he had always been invisible under his hat! He bowed politely.

'You seem to be in difficulties,' he said. 'I am Wise-One the Magician. Can I help you?'

'Yes. Catch the Tiresome Goblin – his hat's bobbing about over there!' yelled Mr. Stamp-About. 'Look – I'll give you this bag of gold if you'll catch him!'

Tiresome took the bag of gold with a grin. He walked up to Billy, who knew him well, of course, and didn't attempt

to butt him.

'Now, now,' said Tiresome, pretending to speak to a goblin, not a goat. 'You can't behave like this. You come along with me!'

The goat allowed himself to be led quietly up the street. When they were far enough away from everyone Tiresome unfastened the hat and took it off the goat's horns. Then Billy the goat followed him back to the busy market place.

'Thanks for the gold!' shouted Tiresome, waving the hat at everyone. 'I'm rich enough not to worry you any more! Good-bye!'

He clapped his hat on his head and became invisible at once. Everyone darted after him, yelling with rage – but Billy the goat met them once again, and they went flying. Oh dear, oh dear, what a terrible morning! They could see that magic hat bobbing away up the street and nobody dared to go after it.

'He's got my money!' wailed Mr. Stamp-About. But as nobody liked him,

nobody felt sorry about that. Mr. Plod wrote a lot of things down in his notebook. 'One day we'll get that goblin,' he said. 'Yes, we will. No doubt about that at all! Please notify me if anyone sees that HAT.'

Well, it's not very likely that we'll see it but you never know. In case you do, here's Mr. Plod's telephone number – PLO 24681357000!

5

Goofy Posts a Letter

'Goofy, go and post this letter for me,' said his aunt, and she gave him a square, white letter, and a little push.

'I want to eat my banana,' said Goofy, who was sitting on the doorstep, just about to begin peeling it.

'You go to the post now, before you miss it,' said his aunt. 'Go along! You can eat your banana when you come back. Leave it on the step.'

But Goofy wasn't going to do that. He felt sure that Scamp the dog would come nosing round. No, he was going to take it down the road with him.

So off he went with the yellow banana and the letter. He didn't hurry. Goofy never did. There were so many things to

see! There was the cat next door washing itself carefully, using its paws for soap and flannel. There was a gardener wheeling his barrow to the rubbish-heap, and Goofy had to stand and watch till the man had tipped everything out.

Then there was the toy shop that had to be looked at, and a big puddle in the road that had to be jumped over two or three times.

Goofy wandered along dreamily, and saw an aeroplane looping the loop in the

sky. He walked with his head in the air watching it, and bumped right into the round, red pillar-box.

'Bother!' said Goofy, and do you know what he did? He posted his big banana! He did, really! It went into the mouth of the box and disappeared – but Goofy quite thought he had posted the letter. That was still in his pocket, of course.

He wandered home again. His aunt saw him and called to him. 'Thank you, Goofy. Did you catch the post?'

'Oh yes,' said Goofy. 'Where's my banana?'

'You took it with you,' said his aunt.

'So I did,' said Goofy. 'But I haven't brought it back. Where is it?'

'You must have eaten it,' said his aunt. Goofy burst into tears. 'Oh, I've eaten it and I didn't know I was eating it! What a waste! Aunt, I ate my lovely banana and I didn't taste it at all! I want another one.'

'Well, you can want,' said his aunt. 'You won't get one out of me by a silly trick like that. You *must* have known you were eating it, Goofy. Don't be silly.'

Goofy was very upset. He hoped he wasn't going to make a habit of eating his food without knowing it. He was very cross and sulky, and nearly got smacked.

He was sent up to bed early because he was rude. His aunt came up to get his trousers to mend. When she picked them up she found something in his pocket – the letter she had given him to post!

How very, very cross she was! 'Look

here, Goofy! You told me you had posted this, and you didn't. You are a very bad boy. Put your clothes on and go straight away and post it for me.'

'I did post your letter, I did, I did,' said Goofy. 'I remember posting it quite well.' All the same he had to go with the letter to the pillar-box down the street, though it meant that his bath water was getting colder and colder.

When he got to the pillar-box the postman was there, talking to the policeman who often walked up and

down Goofy's street.

'And do you know what I found when I cleared this pillar-box last time?' the postman was saying to the big policeman. 'I found a big yellow banana! What do you think of that? Disgraceful, isn't it? And what a waste of a banana. If I catch the person who did that I'll hand him over to you, policeman!'

'Yes, you do,' said the big policeman. 'Time that sort of thing was stopped. Posting bananas, indeed! I suppose people think that because a pillar-box has a mouth it likes to eat!'

Goofy began to shiver and shake. Now he knew where his banana had gone! Oh dear, oh dear, how he hoped the postman would never, never guess that it was *his* banana in the box. He posted his aunt's letter and fled home as if a hundred tigers were after him.

And now he never takes anything out in the street to eat because he's so afraid he might post it again. Poor Goofy, I'm glad I'm not as dreamy as that, aren't you?

6

The Runaway Shoes

There was once a little girl who would keep taking her shoes off in the garden. She liked to feel the grass prickling under her toes; but her mother scolded her and told her a dozen times a day to put her shoes on.

'Alice, there are sharp stones on the path and maybe thorns or prickles in the grass,' she said. 'You might even tread on a bit of broken glass if you run down by the rubbish heap! Then you'd cut your feet badly and be very sorry for yourself.'

But Alice wouldn't obey. So her mother made up her mind to punish her.

'Alice, every time I call and see that you have no shoes on, I shall take tenpence out of your money box to give

to poor children,' she said. 'Then perhaps you'll remember about your shoes.'

Alice was cross. She was saving up for a wheelbarrow, and she didn't want her money to be given away. So she sat in a corner of the garden and sulked.

Then the naughty little girl thought of an idea. 'I know what I'll do,' she said to herself in a whisper. 'I'll take off my shoes and put them just here, behind this stone – and as soon as Mother calls me I'll run and put them on quickly, and Mother will see me running up the garden with my shoes *on*!'

Wasn't she a deceitful little girl? Ah, but wait and see what happened!

The shoes heard what Alice had said. They were shocked, because they were good shoes, and had cost a lot of money. They wanted Alice to behave nicely.

'We know what to do,' whispered the right shoe to the left one. 'As soon as Alice takes us off we'll run away and hide! Then when her mother calls her she won't be able to find us, and she'll get into trouble for being barefooted!'

So as soon as Alice had popped them behind the stone and gone to play in her bare feet, those two shoes kicked up their heels and ran off to hide under the lilac-bush. They couldn't help giggling a bit.

Presently Alice's mother called her: 'Alice! Alice! I want you!'

'Coming, Mother!' called Alice, and ran at once to put on her shoes. But, dear me, they weren't behind the stone. They were gone!

Alice hunted about, but she couldn't find them. Her mother grew angry. 'Alice! Don't you hear me calling? Come at once!'

Alice had to go – and her mother saw she had no shoes on. She was very angry. 'Well, Alice,' she said, 'you must

66

give me tenpence out of your money-box please.'

So Alice had to do this, and she was sad. She ran back down the garden – and there were her shoes just behind the stone again! They had trotted there as soon as Alice had gone up the garden. 'Perhaps she will put us on again now,' they whispered to one another.

But, you know, she didn't! She glared at the shoes and simply could *not* understand how it was that they were behind the stone after all. 'I'm sure you

weren't there just now,' she said. 'Well –
you just stay there now, and I'll be able
to put you on in a hurry if Mother calls
again.'

But you may be sure that as soon as
Alice's back was turned, those two
shoes hopped off again as fast as they
could! They ran to the lilac-bush and
squatted there laughing.

As soon as they heard Alice's mother
again: 'Alice! Alice! Come here!'

Alice rushed to put on her shoes – but

they were gone again, of course. They
weren't behind that stone at all. Alice
was in a dreadful rage. Once again she
had to go to her mother with no shoes
on her feet.

'Alice! You really are a very naughty
little girl,' said her mother. 'That's

another tenpence out of your money-box, please. Well, you won't be able to buy that wheelbarrow if you go on like this.'

Alice ran down the garden, crying. That was a precious twenty pence gone. She suddenly caught sight of her two shoes, sitting quietly behind the stone. She stared and stared. She could *not* understand how it was that they were there now, when she hadn't been able to find them a few minutes ago. It was really very puzzling.

Well, those shoes had a fine game with Alice that morning! Six times they ran off, and six times poor Alice had to go to her mother without her shoes on, and pay tenpence out of her money-box. Now she wouldn't be able to buy the wheelbarrow for ages!

'There's something funny about those shoes,' thought Alice to herself. 'I shall just hide behind the summer-house and watch them.'

So she did – and to her great surprise she saw them galloping off merrily to

The Runaway Shoes

hide under the lilac-bush. She ran after them, calling angrily:

'Shoes! Shoes! Where are you going? You've no right to hide away like that. You've got me into lots of trouble this morning.'

The shoes stopped and turned themselves round. '*We* didn't get you into trouble,' said the right shoe. 'You got yourself into it. If you'd put us on, everything would have been all right.'

'Well! I never knew shoes could talk before!' cried Alice in surprise.

'That shows how silly you are,' said the left shoe. 'You must know perfectly well, Alice, that lace-up shoes have tongues!'

'It's very unkind of you to disobey your mother,' said the left shoe. 'She only wants to save your feet from being cut or scratched. We're going to run away from you every time you take us off in the garden!'

'Then you'll have to give up all your money,' said the right shoe, with a little skip on the grass. 'And serve you right!'

'Well, you just *won't* run away any more!' said Alice angrily, and she took both the shoes into her hands. 'I shall put you on – and keep you on! And you won't be able to play horrid tricks on me any more!'

She put them both on and tied the laces tightly. The shoes grinned at one another.

'We've taught her a lesson,' whispered the right shoe to the left.

'She won't disobey again,' chuckled the left shoe, squeaking as Alice ran

down the garden.

And she didn't! The next time her mother called her, she went at once – with both her shoes on! Her mother was pleased.

'At last you've decided to be a good girl,' she said to Alice. 'Just in time too, or you wouldn't have had a single coin left in your money-box!'

I hope *your* shoes don't run off by themselves. Wouldn't you be surprised.

7

Away it Went

'Mummy, can we go and get two tenpence ice-creams?' said James, putting his head round the door. 'Tessie and I have got some money between us that Uncle Ben gave us yesterday.'

'Yes, if you like,' said Mummy. 'Though how you can eat ice-cream on such a cold day I don't know!'

'Oh, Mummy – we could eat ice-cream if we lived in the middle of a snowstorm!' said Tessie, putting her head round the door, too.

They went off to the dairy to buy two ice creams. Hurray – the notice was up. 'ICES'. It was horrid when the notice said 'No ice-cream today.'

James and Tessie went into the shop and got two cornets. The dairy ices were always so nice and creamy. They went out, carrying them carefully, and began to walk uphill home.

And then something happened. Somebody came flying down the hill on a bicycle, wobbling most dangerously from side to side, followed by a small dog. Tessie and James gave a shout, and jumped to one side. The bicycle flew on, mounted the kerb, wobbled even more, struck a lamp-post and turned over. The little girl riding it was flung off on to her hands and knees.

'Gracious!' said Tessie. 'What a thing to do! Are you hurt?'

The little girl began to howl dismally. Her hands and knees were bleeding. Her little dog ran to her and began to lick her face. She pushed him away.

'My bicycle ran away down the hill,' she sobbed. 'It's broken. And look at my knees and hands! Whatever shall I do?'

'We've got clean hankies,' said Tessie. 'We can bind up your knees, anyway. Your hands aren't too bad. James, where's your hanky?'

James put his ice-cream carefully down on the seat nearby and felt for his hanky. Tessie put her cornet down, too, and got her own hanky out. Then they bound up the little girl's knees for her, and wiped her hands. James tried to straighten the wheel of the bicycle, but it was very, very bent.

'Mummy told me never to ride down the hill,' said the little girl, whose name was Mollie. 'And I did. Serves me right! Thank you for helping. I'll go home now. Where do you live? I shall want to bring back your hankies when Mummy's washed them clean again.'

'At the Red House, up the hill,' said James. They watched the little girl wheel her bicycle away. She turned and whistled for her dog. What was he doing?

Well, perhaps you can guess! He had smelt those ice-creams and eaten both of them up! He was just crunching up Tessie's cornet, when she turned and saw him. She stared in angry dismay.

'You bad dog! Look at him, James – he's gobbled up our ice-creams. Both of

them!'

'*Well* – the horrid little thing!' shouted James, and he looked so fierce that the dog tore off after his little mistress, who was now far down the street with her bicycle.

'It's too bad,' said Tessie, almost in tears. 'We do a good turn, and that dog does us a bad one! I'll never do a good turn again!'

'And nor will I,' said James. 'Fancy having our ice-creams eaten when we've just done something kind. It's not fair.'

They went home angry. They found Mummy and poured out the whole story to her.

'We're never going to be kind again, if that's all the reward we get,' said Tessie. 'You always tell us we must be kind, but what's the good if things like that happen?'

'It's just not fair,' said James. 'It's silly to do good turns. I wouldn't mind if only we got good turns back.'

Mummy didn't look at all pleased. 'You don't do kind things for a reward, surely?' she said. 'You should do them because you want to, or because you just can't help it, or because you know it's the right thing to do. I don't like hearing you talk like this. If you had come and told me your story properly without all this talk of never being kind again and things not being fair, I would have given you money for more ice-creams. As it is, I don't really think you deserve them.'

The children felt ashamed at once. They went red and turned away.

'I won't ask you to do anything for me or to be kind and helpful in future,' said Mummy. 'If that's the way you feel about things, I won't expect you to be kind unless I pay you for it.'

'Oh, Mummy!' said Tessie, almost crying. 'You *know* we love doing things for you. We never expect any reward, though you often give us one. But just to show you we're sorry for the silly things we said, we'll do *all* the jobs you ask us to do, and we *won't* take any reward, even if you offer us one.'

That made Mummy smile. 'Well, we'll see,' she said.

Tessie and James were as good as their word. They ran errands. They tidied the hall cupboard. They cleaned out the henhouse. They even peeled the potatoes one morning when Mummy was busy. And they wouldn't take any reward at all!

They often talked about the little girl and the bicycle. 'It's funny she didn't bring back our hankies, isn't it?' said Tessie. 'She ought to have done that. It is horrid to lose our hankies *and* our ice-creams!'

And then one day they passed a house and heard someone tapping loudly at the window there. They looked and it was the little girl who had fallen off the bicycle! She disappeared, and came running out of the front door, followed by her mother.

'Oh, I've been looking everywhere for you! I forgot where you said you lived. I've got your hankies all nice and clean for you. And Mummy wants you to

come to our party next week, if we ask
your mother if you may. Will you?'

This was all said in one breath, with
the little girl dancing round like mad, and
her little dog racing about, and her
mother smiling all over her face.

'Tell me your names and where you
live and I'll telephone your mother and
ask her if you can come to Mollie's
party,' said Mollie's mother. 'She's going
to have a conjurer – and crackers – and
ice-creams . . .'

'Oooooh!' said Tessie and James.

82

Away it Went

That was the kind of party they loved. They took the clean hankies, talked to Mollie for a while then raced off to tell their mother all about it.

'Well!' said Mummy, 'I am glad. You deserve it, because you've done so many, many kind things for me this week and done them for love, instead of a reward. You didn't even expect one. And now, quite unexpectedly, here comes a lovely treat for you both. You really do deserve it!'

They went to Mollie's party, of course – and you'll hardly believe it, but they had four ice-creams each!

'We lost one ice-cream – but we've had *four* this afternoon,' said James to Tessie. 'I *am* sorry we made such a fuss, aren't you? I never will again!'

I think they had a very sensible mother, don't you? I expect you've got one like that too.

8

The Strange Little Boy

Sammy was a strange little boy. He didn't seem to have any kindness in him! He didn't feel sorry when he saw somebody hurt, and he only laughed when his little sister fell down and cut her knee.

'One day, Sammy,' said his mother, 'you'll fall down yourself, and then you'll not want to be laughed at. You'll want me to comfort you and bandage your knee.'

'Pooh!' said Sammy. 'I'm not so silly as to fall down!'

It was quite true that Sammy never fell down. He was a very careful boy, and not since he had been a baby had he fallen down at all. He was so careful that he had never cut himself with a knife, never pricked himself with a pin, and never even bumped his head.

Well, he was very lucky, but good luck like that can't last for ever, as you'll see.

Sammy went to school one morning, running along with Ellen his sister. She tried to jump over a puddle, and down she went on to her knees. She made them both bleed, and how she cried!

'Cry-baby!' said Sammy, unkindly. 'You're silly to fall down, and sillier still to make that noise. Be quiet!'

'Oh, Sammy, my knees do hurt!' sobbed his little sister. 'Do take me into school and bathe them for me and tie them up.'

'I shan't,' said Sammy. 'I'm sure you're making a fuss, Ellen. They'll be all right in a minute.'

'Sammy, you are unkind,' said Freda, who was in Sammy's class. 'Come along, Ellen. I'll take you in.'

The next thing that happened was in the handwork class. The boy next to Sammy was working with a sharp pocket-knife, and suddenly his hand slipped. He cut his thumb badly, and it hurt him. The tears came into his eyes.

'Baby!' said Sammy. 'Cry-baby! You should be more careful! *I* never cut myself!'

'Will you tie it up for me?' said the boy, sucking his thumb.

'Good gracious! Tie up a little cut like that! I wouldn't bother with it,' said Sammy, who didn't want to stop his work. So the boy went to ask the teacher, and was sent to bathe the cut. Everyone thought Sammy was very unkind.

Well, the third thing that happened was that Winnie bumped her head hard against the edge of the open cupboard door. Goodness, what a bang it was!

Winnie stood there, blinking her eyes, trying not to cry, her face very red indeed. She rubbed the bump. 'Good gracious!' she said bravely. 'I *have* got a dreadful lump on my head now. Feel, Sammy.'

Sammy felt. It was a very big bump

indeed – but the unkind boy only laughed.

'It serves you right for being so silly!' he said. 'Why don't you look around you properly, then you won't keep bumping your head?'

'My mother would put something cool on the bump,' said Winnie, feeling upset to hear Sammy's unkind words. 'She would rub butter on it.'

'What a waste of butter!' said Sammy. 'Don't make a fuss, Winnie! Good gracious, the fusses you all make about falling down, and cutting yourselves, and bumping your heads! And then you expect people to be kind to you after you've been so silly. You should do as I do and not go about hurting yourselves every day!'

Ah, wait, Sammy! Nobody can say things like that without having something happen to them!

And it happened that very morning in the playground. It was playtime at eleven o'clock, and the boys and girls were having a game of catch. Sammy was out of breath, and he stood by the school gate, which was open so that the bigger children might go into the school garden from the playground, and weed or dig if they wanted to.

Well, Sammy stood there, panting, his fingers holding the gate-post – and suddenly the wind blew roughly and the gate slammed shut, right on to poor Sammy's fingers!

Poor, poor Sammy! You know how dreadful it is to pinch or trap your fingers, don't you? Much worse than bumping your head or cutting your knee! Well, that's what happened to Sammy that morning in the playground.

He screamed. Someone opened the gate and set his fingers free, but they hurt so much that they didn't feel like fingers at all. And then Sammy the bold and the careful, Sammy the brave, Sammy the unkind, began to cry and sob as if he were five years old like Ellen.

'He's trapped his fingers!' said John. 'Dear me, don't make such a fuss, Sammy! That's what you tell us.'

'Cry-baby!' said Winnie.

'How careless of you!' said Freda.

'Oh, oh, my poor fingers!' wept Sammy. 'Oh, can't somebody help me? Oh, my fingers!'

The children stood round looking at Sammy. It was the first time they had seen him cry.

'You are always unkind and hard to us, Sammy,' said Freda. 'How do you like it when we laugh at *you*, and won't help you? Cry-baby!'

The Strange Little Boy

But then up came little Ellen, Sammy's sister, her knees still bandaged with Freda's hankies. She ran to Sammy.

'Sammy! What's the matter?'

'I've pinched my poor fingers in the gate,' wept Sammy. 'Oh, oh, they hurt dreadfully! Oh, Ellen, what can I do?'

The little girl looked round at the children, who were nudging each other and laughing at Sammy, very glad to see the unkind boy in such a fix. The little girl was angry.

'How can you stand here laughing at poor Sammy!' she cried. 'Oh, you *are* unkind!'

'Well, he's always unkind to us,' said Freda. 'He laughed at you when you fell down this morning, Ellen.'

'I don't care!' cried Ellen fiercely. 'Because somebody is unkind to me isn't any reason why I should be unkind too. How can you teach people to be kind if you're unkind to them yourself? I think you're all horrid! I'm sorry for poor Sammy and his hurt fingers.'

Sammy sobbed and sobbed. His

fingers hurt him just as much as ever, and the pain wouldn't go away. The other children began to look uncomfortable. They weren't really unkind, but they couldn't help feeling glad that Sammy had been punished.

'Don't cry, Sammy,' said Freda suddenly in a softer voice. She put her arm round him. It was lovely to Sammy to feel someone loving him when he was so unhappy.

'Poor old Sammy,' said John. 'Can't we do something?'

'My poor fingers,' wept Sammy.

'*I* know how to make the pain better,' said Winnie suddenly. 'I knew all the time, but I was feeling unkind and I didn't say anything. Come along, Sammy. I'll show you what to do.'

She slipped her arm round him and led the little boy to the cloakroom where there was a basin and taps. She turned on the cold-water tap, and the water ran icy cold.

'Put your fingers under the tap and let the icy water run over them,' said

Winnie. 'That's what my mother makes me do when I pinch my fingers. It takes the pain away.'

So Sammy put his hurt fingers under the tap and let the cold water run over them – and oh, how lovely, the pain went away and he could soon move his fingers properly again. He wiped his eyes and stopped crying.

'We're sorry we were unkind to you, Sammy,' said Freda. 'We know how dreadful it is when you hurt yourself, and nobody comforts you. Do you feel better now?'

'Yes, thank you,' said Sammy. He wiped his tear-stained face again and looked round at the others. 'I know how you must all have felt when I laughed at you. I'll never do it again. It was so nice of you to be kind to me – I know I didn't deserve it. But I'll pay you back for your kindness – especially you, Winnie.'

And do you suppose he kept his word? Yes, you're right – he did. The first person that runs to help anyone who has fallen down is Sammy! The one who

The Strange Little Boy

uses his clean hanky to bandage hurt knees is Sammy! He'll slip his arm round you if you're unhappy – and my goodness, if you pinch your fingers, Sammy's as good as a doctor or a mother!

He had a hard lesson to learn, but he learnt it well. Good old Sammy!

9

Mr. Wibble-Wobble

Jiminy was a naughty little boy-doll. He was so mischievous that the other toys wouldn't have anything to do with him.

'You're mean!' said Jiminy. 'You've got some sweets and you won't share them with me. You've made some cakes on the little toy stove, but you won't give me any. I don't like you.'

'Oh, we don't mind,' said the toy dog. 'We don't mind at all! The more you dislike us and keep away from us the better we'll be pleased. You're a nuisance.'

'You undid the door of my ark and let all the animals out last night,' said Mr. Noah. 'I had a dreadful time getting them all back.'

'And you tied my tail into a knot when I was asleep,' said the clockwork mouse.

'And you stole the ribbon off my hair

when *I* was asleep,' said the little blue-eyed doll. 'Oh, don't tell me you didn't. I can see you're wearing it for a scarf round your neck.'

'So keep away from us, because we certainly shan't give you any cakes or sweets,' said the panda. 'And you won't get any of the lemonade we're going to make tonight, either.'

Jiminy was angry. He scowled. Horrid things! If only he could get the sweets and buns and lemonade *somehow*!

He went into the toy cupboard and sulked. Nobody came near him. He got tired of sulking and began to look into the boxes piled at the back – and he came across a little flat rubber thing.

'Ah!' said Jiminy to himself, 'I know what this is. It's a balloon! I've seen the children blow them up. I wonder if I could blow *this* up!'

He tried. He blew and he blew. The balloon began to swell. Jiminy couldn't blow it up as much as it should have been blown up, but still he made it quite

big. He tied a bit of string round the neck.

And then he got a shock. The balloon had a face on it! It was only painted on, of course, but still, it was certainly a face, and it was rather surprising to see it on a balloon.

Jiminy looked at it. Then he grinned a little secret grin all to himself. He would play a trick on the toys - and he would make them give him everything he wanted. Aha, toys, look out! You're in for a very bad time.

Jiminy hunted about till he found a long red coat belonging to an old doll that no longer lived in the nursery. He buttoned it tightly over his head - yes, right over the top of his head, so that his face couldn't be seen. And in the neck of the coat he pulled the neck of the balloon, and held it tightly by the string.

How peculiar he looked – how very, very peculiar! He stepped out of the toy cupboard, the coat hanging down to his ankles, the big balloon-face wobbling in the neck of the coat looking very extraordinary indeed.

'Good evening!' said Jiminy, in a very deep voice. The toys all looked round at once. There was a dead silence when

101

they saw the balloon-face looking at them over the top of the long coat.

'Ooooh! I don't like it!' said the blue-eyed doll, suddenly. 'Who is it?'

'I'm Mr. Wibble-Wobble,' said Jiminy, enjoying himself. He made the balloon-face wobble a bit, and the panda ran behind the wastepaper basket in fright. 'I've come to share your buns and lemonade.'

'Who told you we had any?' said the teddy bear.

'My friend, Jiminy,' said Mr. Wibble-Wobble, and wobbled his head again in a most terrifying manner. 'Give me some, please, or I shall wobble over to you and eat you.'

The blue-eyed doll gave a scream and ran to the teddy bear. She clutched him hard.

'Give him some buns, give him them all!' she begged him. 'I don't want to be eaten, I don't, I don't.'

'And some lemonade, please,'said Mr. Wibble-Wobble, in his deep voice. 'And what about a few sweets?'

'I don't see why you should have *any*,' said the bear, boldly. 'Just because you are a friend of Jiminy's – I never heard of such a thing!'

Mr. Wibble-Wobble took two or three steps towards the teddy bear, and the blue-eyed doll squealed again. She ran to the toy stove and took a tin of buns from the oven. She thrust them at Mr. Wibble-Wobble.

'Here you are, here you are – now go away, you horrid, wobbly thing!'

'Now the sweets and lemonade,' said

103

Mr. Wibble-Wobble, and his grinning balloon-face shook to and fro.

'I don't see why he should have our things,' said the teddy bear. 'Panda, don't let's give him any more.'

'I shall want your bow from round your neck,' said Mr. Wibble-Wobble, in a very fierce voice. 'And, panda, I shall want your coat. Take it off.'

'Certainly not,' said the panda, in rather a trembling voice. Mr. Wibble-Wobble began to do a most peculiar dance, his head wobbling all the time. He got nearer and nearer to the panda, who suddenly took off his coat and threw it to Mr. Wibble-Wobble in fright.

'Soldiers, soldiers, help, help!' called the blue-eyed doll. 'Come out of your box, oh, do, do, do!'

The lid of the soldiers' box lifted, and the captain looked out. He was very surprised to see Mr. Wibble-Wobble.

'Ho!' said Mr. Wibble-Wobble, 'I'll have your sword, Captain! Present it to me, please.'

'Certainly not!' thundered the Captain,

and he leapt out of the box, but when he saw Mr. Wibble-Wobble wobbling over to him, he was frightened.

He threw his sword at him, shouting: 'All right, take it – but don't come any nearer. Take it.'

The sharp sword flew straight at the balloon-face. It pricked it – and there was a tremendous BANG! The toys all fell down flat. So did Jiminy, because he got a terrible shock, too.

The teddy-bear looked out of one eye at Mr. Wibble-Wobble, wondering what

105

had happened – goodness gracious, his head was gone! It had disappeared. Where in the world was it?

And then out from the neck of the coat came Jiminy's scared face – where was the balloon? What had happened to it? What was that terrific BANG?

'Oh, oh – it was Jiminy after all! It wasn't Mr. Wibble-Wobble!' yelled the bear, and he ran over to Jiminy and pummelled him hard. Soon all the toys were doing the same, and Jiminy shouted for mercy.

'You won't get any mercy!' cried the blue-eyed doll. 'Mr. Wibble-Wobble didn't show us any!'

And poor Jiminy had hard work to creep back into the toy cupboard and hide himself away. He won't do any mischief for a long, long time – and he just can't make out where that balloon went to. He's really not very clever, is he?

10

Oh, You Greedy Dog!

Rip was greedy. He was a big dog with a big appetite, and he had plenty to eat. But he didn't think so!

'I'm starved!' he said, and he went round to people's back doors and looked up at them so sadly out of his brown eyes that they rushed indoors and brought him out bones and scraps of meat and pudding dishes to lick round.

He even stole dinners put down for all the cats round about. The big tabby was cross, because she did enjoy her bowl of bread and milk - and when Rip came along it was gone in a minute!

The black cat wished her mistress wouldn't put her dinner down outside the back door, because as soon as Rip smelt it he was there in a flash - and her

dinner disappeared in a flash, too!

'You are a mean, greedy dog,' she scolded and she spat at him, wishing she dared to put her claws into him. But she didn't because he was so big.

'It's your own fault,' said Rip, licking his lips. 'You should eat more quickly - you're so slow.'

'All cats are slow in eating,' said the black cat. 'We have good manners. We don't gobble like dogs.'

Everyone knew how greedy Rip was, especially the children. Sometimes they brought him old bones just to see him crunch them all up one by one and swallow them. He seemed to be able to go on for ever!

Now, one day two men wanted to burgle the house where Rip lived. 'We'll choose a night when the owners are out,' said one.

'What about the dog?' asked the other. 'He'll bark like anything.'

'That doesn't matter. There's nobody much to hear him round there,' said the first man. 'The thing is - will he go for

us? Is he kept loose in the yard, or is he on a chain?'

'Loose,' said the other man. 'And he's a big dog, too. He has a kennel in the yard.'

'Is he the dog that's so greedy?' said the first man, after a pause.

'Yes. But I don't see how that helps us – unless you're thinking of giving him poisoned meat or something,' said the other. 'And I can't agree to that. I like dogs.'

'I *wasn't* thinking of that,' said his

friend. 'Of course not. But I've got another idea. I don't know if it would work.'

'What?' said his friend.

'Well - what about taking sacks of biscuits and bones and titbits with us,' said the first man, 'and throwing them into his kennel? If he's as greedy as everyone says he is, he'll gobble the lot - and he'll be so fat that he won't be able to get out of his kennel - kennel doors are always very small, to keep out the wind.'

'It's an idea,' said his friend. 'But I don't know if it'll work. We'll try it.'

Well, you should have seen them the next night, taking along bags and packets of food for Rip - bones, biscuits, stale buns from the baker's, scraps from the butcher, titbits of all kinds! They came to the yard where Rip was running about loose. He growled.

The men leaned over the wall near his kennel, and threw half a dozen buns into it. Rip was after the buns at once. He gobbled them all up. The men threw

in some bones – and then handfuls of biscuits. Rip was thrilled. What very, very nice kind men! As long as they kept to the other side of the wall he wouldn't even bark.

They threw in the scraps of meat. Rip snapped them all up. Then he ate six more stale buns and a whole lot of tasty titbits. Well, well, well – what an appetite! The men marvelled to see it! They tried to see if Rip had got any fatter, but it was dark in the kennel, and they couldn't see a thing.

114

'I'll climb over into the yard – and if he comes shooting out after me, you must pull me back again quickly,' said one of the men. 'We've no more food for him, so we must just chance it now.'

He hopped over the wall. Rip saw him and growled at once. Then he bared his teeth and snarled. The man stood there and watched him, ready to fling himself back over the wall if necessary. Rip tried to rush out of his kennel to attack him.

But what was this? He couldn't get out! He stuck in the middle of the kennel opening, and he couldn't get out any farther! He was so dreadfully fat with all his buns and bones and biscuits that he simply couldn't squeeze through.

'It's all right – he's stuck!' said the man to his friend. 'Quick, come on. We can do the job nicely now.'

Both men went over to the house and forced open a window. Rip barked like mad and struggled to get out of his kennel. It wasn't a bit of good. He couldn't understand it. Why couldn't he

get out as he usually did?

The men disappeared into the house. Rip knew they were up to no good and he barked again. How he wanted to snap at those men and bite them! But he couldn't.

He had to stand there, half in and half out of his kennel, tired out with struggling and barking.

The tabby cat came curiously into his yard. 'What is the matter?' she said. 'Why did you bark?'

'Robbers,' said Rip, anxiously. 'And I

couldn't get out of my kennel. Why couldn't I, Tabby?'

The cat went to his kennel and peered in. She could see quite well in the dark. She laughed.

'If you could see yourself! You're as fat as a pig! No wonder you couldn't get out. Whatever have you been eating?'

Rip groaned. 'Oh my – I ate everything those men gave me. It was a trick – they meant to make me so fat that I couldn't go for them. Whatever will my master say?'

His master said a great deal. When he got home and found his house broken into, and his goods stolen, he went out to Rip with a whip.

'What do you suppose I keep you for, and feed you well for?' he cried. 'Aren't you a watch-dog? Don't I trust you? Well, you're not to be trusted and I'm ashamed of you. I shall whip you, and hope that will teach you to guard my house properly next time. And what's more, you won't get fed so well – you don't deserve it!'

Oh, You Greedy Dog!

Poor Rip. He knew he deserved the whipping, and he was very sad. And now he isn't nearly so fat because he doesn't get so much food. He doesn't even go round asking for any, or stealing the cats' dinners. He has never, never forgotten that dreadful night when he was so greedy that he made himself too fat to squeeze out of his kennel!

11

A Peculiar Adventure

'Miaow!' said a voice, just down by Ronnie's feet. He looked down, but he couldn't see anything, which wasn't very surprising because there was a thick fog that hid even the houses nearby.

'Where are you?' said Ronnie. 'You're a cat, I suppose, and you're lost in the fog.'

'MIAOW!' said the cat in a louder voice, and rubbed itself against Ronnie's legs. He switched on his torch and looked down.

'My word! What a wonderful cat you are!' he said. 'As black as soot, and with eyes as green as cucumbers. Are you lost? Where do you live?'

'Miaow-ee-ow-ee-ow,' said the cat, as if

it was explaining where its home was.
Then Ronnie noticed that it wore a little
collar round its neck with a disc
hanging from it. Perhaps its name and
address were on that. He looked at the
disc in the light of his torch.

cinders
Wizard Cottage
Hanger
Lane

'Yes – here's your name, I suppose – Cinders – and your address – Wizard Cottage, Hanger Lane. Well, Hanger Lane isn't far away, Cinders, so I'll take you there and find your house. Wizard Cottage! What a strange name for a house. I've never noticed it before. Come along. Keep at my heels and we'll soon be there.'

The cat kept close to Ronnie as he went down the road and round the corner. The little boy flashed his torch on the name on each gate.

'Holly Trees. That's not it. Little Abbey. That's not it, either. What's this one? Red Roofs. I do hope we shan't have to go all down the road before we find it, and then back again down the opposite side!'

'Miaow!' said the cat. Ronnie went on down the road, looking for Wizard Cottage – and there it was, the very, very last house in the row, the one on the corner. Its name was on the gate: Wizard Cottage.

'Here we are,' said Ronnie. 'Shall I

ring the bell and hand you in, puss? If I leave you wandering about outside you may get lost again. I'll ring or knock.'

He knocked, because there was no bell. The knocker was very strange. It was in the shape of a hand, and Ronnie felt as if it was shaking hands with him when he knocked.

The door opened, but nobody stood behind it. Ronnie hesitated. He didn't like to go in. But the cat walked straight in, turned round and looked at Ronnie.

'Miaow!' it said politely.

'DO COME IN!' shouted a voice. 'And shut the door. The fog's spoiling my work.'

Ronnie went in and shut the door. He walked up a very long passage and found himself in a perfectly round room.

124

He stared in amazement.

A fire with green flames came up from a hole in the middle of the floor! Over it hung a great golden pot in which something boiled and bubbled, singing an odd little tune the whole time. A tall man in a flowing black cloak and a high-pointed hat was pouring something into the pot.

The cat ran up to him and rubbed itself against his legs.

'So you've come back, Cinders!' he said. 'Didn't I tell you not to go out into

A Peculiar Adventure

the fog? You're too late to help me now, and I don't feel at all pleased with you.'

'Er – please excuse me,' said Ronnie, feeling puzzled and excited. 'I found your lost cat, and brought him back.'

'Oh – I'm sorry I didn't see you,' said the tall man, turning round with a smile that lighted up his whole face and made Ronnie like him very much. 'You came in with Cinders, I suppose. Thank you for looking after him. He's no good in a fog, but he will go out in them.'

Ronnie didn't know what to say. He stared at the bubbling pot, and was astonished to see the liquid in it change suddenly from green to yellow and then to a bright silver.

'Excuse me a moment. I really must stir this,' said the man. 'By the way I must introduce myself, mustn't I? I'm Mr. Spells.'

'I'm Ronnie James,' said Ronnie.

'Miaow,' said the cat.

'Don't keep interrupting,' said Mr. Spells. 'Oh, you want some milk, do you? Ronnie, stir this mixture for me, will you, and I'll get Cinders some milk.'

Ronnie found himself stirring the strange bubbling mixture. Some of it splashed on the edge of the pot on to his right shoe.

'Oh, dear – what a good thing I've got my very oldest shoes on,' said Ronnie. 'Mr. Spells – what is this mixture you're making?'

'Oh, just some invisible paint,' said Mr. Spells. 'Once it cools, you can use it on anything, and it makes any object invisible. You can't see it, you know,

when you've dabbed it with this. Very useful sometimes.'

Ronnie began to tremble. Was this man a wizard? His house was called Wizard Cottage – and his name was Mr. Spells. He had a black cat, too, as all witches and wizards had.

'You needn't be afraid of me,' said Mr. Spells kindly. 'I can see you trembling. There are bad wizards and good ones, just as there are bad boys and good boys. Well, I'm a good wizard. I hope you're a good boy?'

'Mother says I am,' said Ronnie, still trembling a little. Then he heard a clock strike five. 'Oh, dear – is it really five o'clock? I must go, then, because Mother will worry if I don't get back in time. She'll think I'm lost in the fog.'

'Well, thank you again for bringing Cinders home,' said Mr. Spells. 'Perhaps you will come and have tea with me tomorrow? I'd be delighted to see you. I could teach you quite a lot of interesting things.'

'Oh, *thank* you! I'd love to come to

tea!' said Ronnie delighted. 'I'll be along at half-past four after school. Goodbye, Mr. Spells. Goodbye, Cinders.'

'Miaow,' said Cinders. Ronnie stroked him and then went down the passage and let himself out of the front door. He walked home in the fog, feeling quite dazed. What a very peculiar adventure! And to think he was going to tea with Mr. Spells the next day – with a *wizard*! He *must* be a wizard – how very exciting!

His mother laughed when he told her about his adventure. 'You've been dreaming in the fog!' she said. 'But go if you like – and just ask Mr. Spells if he can give me a bit of magic to keep the fire from going out. It's behaving very badly lately!'

So the next afternoon Ronnie set off. He went all the way down Hanger Lane to the corner – but dear me, what was this? The house at the corner was called Thornfield, not Wizard Cottage. Then

where was Wizard Cottage? It should be next to Thornfield, on the corner.

But it wasn't. There was no house beyond Thornfield. It was a very puzzling thing. No matter how hard Ronnie hunted he simply could not find Wizard Cottage.

'Well, all I can think is that Mr. Spells must have painted his house with his invisible paint!' thought Ronnie. 'I'll just have to keep a look-out for old Cinders I might see him and get him to take me into the house again some day.'

Ronnie's mother wasn't a bit surprised to see Ronnie coming home without having found the house. 'It was all nonsense!' she said. 'You made it up – or dreamt it.'

But now I'll tell you a very peculiar thing. Do you remember that some of the mixture in the pot splashed over on to Ronnie's right shoe? Well, when it cooled it made the whole shoe invisible! So now Ronnie can't see it, and he's been hunting high and low for it.

And it's there in his cupboard, lying beside the left shoe, but it can't be seen! You might tell him, if you see him.

12

The Doll that wanted a Mother

'I don't like my mother,' said Goldilocks, the walking doll. She was talking to a doll who sat on the park-seat beside her.

The other doll looked shocked. 'Don't like your mother! What a dreadful thing to say! Which little girl is she? Tell me.'

'Well, do you see that child over there, in the brown coat and red shirt?' said Goldilocks. 'The one with straight brown hair? She's my mother. She's horrid.'

'Oh dear, I *do* feel sorry for you,' said the other doll. 'That's *my* mother over there – the little girl with golden curls. She's so kind and sweet, and will you believe it, when she goes to bed at night she always undresses me first and puts

me into my cot and tucks me up.'

'You're lucky,' said Goldilocks. 'I never get tucked up. Or kissed and hugged. But I get plenty of smacks.'

The dolls talked away to one another. All dolls look upon little girls they belong to as their mothers, and just as in the real grown-up mother world, there are good and bad mothers, so there are good and bad mothers in the little-girl world.

And poor Goldilocks had a very bad one indeed. 'She's so unkind,' said

Goldilocks. 'She pulls all her toys about and breaks them. She shouts and screams if things go wrong, and then we all try to get out of her way because she slaps us. I really haven't got a proper mother – not like you have, to tuck me up at night and love me.'

'Why don't you go and look for one?' said the other doll. 'You're a walking doll, aren't you? I'll wind you up when nobody's looking, if you like, and you can slip down from the seat and walk quietly away.'

'Well, wait till it's getting dark,' said Goldilocks, feeling excited. 'Then I shan't be seen so easily. It gets dark at tea time now, and I can slip away before my mother collects me.'

So when it was beginning to get dark, and the children in the park were thinking of going home, the doll wound up Goldilocks. Down to the ground she stepped and began walking quickly along the path.

A nurse saw her and was most astonished. But she couldn't go after her

because she had a baby in a pram. Then a little boy saw her and was frightened. Next a dog saw her and ran up to sniff. What could this strange little walking animal be?

Goldilocks didn't like the dog at all. One snap and her head would be bitten off. But the dog gave her a wet lick and disappeared. He thought she was a little girl who had become very small.

Then the park policeman saw her and called to her to stop. 'Hey there, you! Who are you? What are you doing all by yourself?'

Goldilocks didn't answer. She ran under a seat and hid till the policeman had gone by. She didn't want to be captured.

She ran on. She came to a car standing by the side of the road. One of the doors was open. Goldilocks peeped inside. A little girl was there, reading.

'Please,' said Goldilocks, 'can you take me home? I'm a walking doll and I'm very unhappy because I'm lost.'

The little girl looked up in surprise. 'Gracious! A doll that can walk *and* talk! No, I shan't take you back to your home! I'll have you for myself and show you off to all my friends!'

She made a grab at the doll, but Goldilocks jumped to the kerb and ran for her life. Goodness! That little girl

would never do for a mother! What a hard, unkind little face she had!

Goldilocks walked on again, down a path and in at a gate. She came to a door. It was ajar. She walked in and listened for children's voices. Ah, there were some upstairs. Perhaps she would find a mother here.

Up she went, and peered round the door. She saw three little girls there, playing Ludo.

'Please,' said Goldilocks, 'will you take me home? I'm a walking doll and

The Doll that wanted a Mother

I'm very unhappy because I'm lost.'

All the little girls looked up in the greatest surprise.

'A live doll!' said one little girl. 'I've never seen one before. I'll have you, little doll.'

'No, you won't. I shall have her,' said the second child.

'I'm the oldest so she shall belong to *me*,' said the third one. And then the first child slapped the third one and the second child threw the counters at them both!

That was quite enough for Goldilocks! She ran down the stairs as fast as she could go. Three spiteful mothers – that would never do!

She went out of the gate and wandered down the road. Soon she met another little girl wheeling a doll's pram. 'Please,' said Goldilocks, 'will you take me home? I'm a walking doll and I'm very unhappy because I'm lost.'

'Good gracious!' said the little girl. She picked Goldilocks up and put her in the pram. 'I never heard of such a strange thing. Now you stay there just a minute whilst I take this note to the lady in this house.'

She disappeared through the gate. A small voice spoke from the pram. 'Are you really a walking, talking doll? Well, I advise you not to ask Lulu to be your mother! She's like the little girl in the rhyme, the one who had a curl in the middle of her forehead – when she's good she's very, very good, but when she's bad she's horrid! She's got a bad temper, you know, and bad-tempered

143

people aren't good mothers.'

'Oh – thank you for telling me,' said Goldilocks, and she scrambled down from the pram. 'I don't want a bad-tempered mother. I want a mother who will always love me, one I can really trust.'

She ran off before the little girl came back – and she bumped straight into another girl carrying a bag of shopping. Neither of them saw the other in the dark, and Goldilocks fell over and bumped her head. She began to cry.

The little girl was astonished. She carried Goldilocks to a street lamp and looked at her. She took out her handkerchief and wiped the doll's face and fussed over her.

'Did I hurt you? I'm sorry. What are you? Surely you must be a fairy, though you look like a doll! But I've never seen a doll that walked and talked before!'

'Please,' sobbed Goldilocks, 'will you take me home? I'm very unhappy because I'm lost.'

'You poor little thing,' said Alice, the

little girl. 'Of course, I'll take you home. I'd simply *love* to keep you myself, because you're really wonderful – but that would be unkind, because you want to go home to your mother.'

'I *don't* want to go home!' said Goldilocks, smiling through her tears. 'I ran away because I have a horrid mother. I'm trying to find a new one, a kind one. So I've been begging each little girl I meet to take me home, just to see if I could find one who was kind enough to say she would. Then I knew she would be a good mother!'

'Well! Fancy that!' said Alice. 'I'll be
your mother, then, and you shall belong
to me. I've four dolls already, but I've
got enough love for lots more. You come
home now, and I'll get a bed ready for
you, and you shall make friends with all
the other toys.'

So Goldilocks went off very happily
with Alice – and if you meet a little girl
who has five dolls called Angela,
Josephine, Amelia, Rosebud – and
Goldilocks – you'll know who she is.
She'll be Alice, the mother Goldilocks
set out to find.

13

He was a bit too Quick

Whenever any of the three children had a sore throat Mother always made them a cup of blackcurrant tea. It was lovely. She took out a pot of blackcurrant jam, put a big spoonful into a cup, and then poured boiling water on to it. She stirred in some sugar, and when the blackcurrant tea was cooling, it made a really lovely drink.

'It's almost worth while having a sore throat to be able to drink a cup of Mother's blackcurrant tea,' said Judy. 'And my throat is *always* better after it. Always.'

'So's mine,' said Jack, and Pat said the same. When George, their cousin, came to stay with them they told him about the blackcurrant tea, too.

147

'Judy's just had a bad throat, and Mother made her some blackcurrant tea,' said Pat. 'It made her throat *much* better – so Mother gave her another cup of it, and after that her throat was well. It's simply lovely stuff.'

Now, George was an artful boy and very greedy, too. He thought that blackcurrant tea made from jam would be a lovely thing to have – much nicer than lemonade. But what a pity to have to wait for a sore throat before he could have any!

And then he suddenly had one of his ideas! He could easily *pretend* he had a sore throat.

'If I go around coughing a bit, and saying my throat hurts, Aunt Susan will be sure to give me blackcurrant tea,' he thought. So he put on a silly little cough, and looked miserable.

'My throat hurts,' he told the others. They told their mother. She looked at George, and remembered that he had eaten a most enormous dinner and that she had herd him yelling like a Red Indian immediately afterwards. He couldn't be ill if he ate like that and certainly he wouldn't yell at the top of his voice if his throat was hurting him so much.

She was used to George and his artful ways. 'I don't think George has much of a throat,' she said.

'I should like some blackcurrant tea to make it better,' said George at once, and coughed.

'Well, we'll see how you are after tea,' said his aunt. 'I don't waste my

blackcurrant tea on anyone who *hasn't* a bad throat, you know.'

George scowled. Then he made himself cough so much that his throat really began to feel quite sore!

His aunt took no notice, but went out of the room. 'I think your mother's unkind,' said George to Pat.

'She's not,' said Pat, at once. 'I expect she's gone to get the blackcurrant jam. You'll find it all ready for you to drink soon.'

George hoped Pat was right. He

waited for his aunt to come back, but she didn't. He went up to his bedroom, took down a book, and sulked over it for a long time. Horrid Aunt Susan! His mother always made such a fuss of him if he so much as pricked his finger.

After some time he went downstairs to find the others. They had gone out for a walk. George went into the kitchen, scowling and cross. How horrid everyone was!

But then his face brightened. In the middle of the table was a cup of some

purplish stuff – blackcurrant tea, thought George. Was it for him? Well, he'd drink it anyhow, whether it was for him or not. It looked lovely!

He tipped up the cup and drank the purple liquid straight off. He put the empty cup down and made a face. Ooooooh! What a nasty taste! Well, if that was blackcurrant tea *he* certainly didn't want any more! How simply disgusting! However could the others like it so much? It wasn't even sweet.

He decided not to say anything more about his throat at all, in case his aunt offered him some more of that horrible tea. So when the others came home he announced that he was quite well again and ready for a game.

'Is your throat better then?' said Judy, in surprise.

'Yes, I drank a cup of your mother's blackcurrant tea and it got quite well,' said George. 'What game shall we play now?'

'Pat doesn't feel very like a game,' said Judy. '*She's* got a sore throat now!

It came on when we were out. She's gone to ask Mother for some blackcurrant tea.'

Soon Pat came in with her mother. She held a cup full of purplish stuff in her hand. George shuddered. He looked at his aunt. She carried a cup, too.

'Here you are, George,' she said, holding it out to him. 'Drink this. You asked me for it before. It will be good for your throat.'

'No thank you, Aunt Susan,' said George. I've already had one cup of blackcurrant tea, and it's made my throat QUITE better!'

His aunt stared at him in surprise. 'Who gave you the tea? I haven't made any till now.'

'I found a cup of it on the table there,' said George. 'It was delicious, Aunt Susan. I drank it all up – and my throat's better.'

To his surprise, Judy, Jack and Pat suddenly began to scream with laughter. Mother was surprised too.

'Oh, dear – what *do* you think George

has done?' cried Judy at last. 'We painted in our painting books this afternoon – and when we went out we cleared up except for the paint-water. We left it in a cup on the table – and George must have thought it was blackcurrant tea and drank it up! Oh, *George!*'

George went scarlet. His aunt laughed and laughed, and the others clutched each other and roared helplessly.

'He drank our dirty painting-water.'

'Was it lovely, George?'

'Have some more?'

'Well, George,' said his aunt, 'I'm very, very glad to hear that you've cured your bad throat with a dose of painting-water. How clever of you! I shall know what to give you next time you have a bad throat.'

So now poor George never dares to say he has a cold just in case his aunt remembers what she said and gives him painting-water to drink. Well, he shouldn't have pretended, should he?

14

At Rushy Bridge

Every day little Tricky, the elf, went shopping for his mother. He went across the fields to Rushy Bridge, and over the bridge to the village.

Rushy Bridge was just one plank thrown across the stream, which was very wide just there. Tricky liked to stop in the middle and look down at himself in the water.

Big-Toes, the imp, watched Tricky coming back from shopping each day. Sometimes Tricky had a big cake, sometimes he had the newspapers, sometimes he had a basket of groceries.

'He's frightened of me!' said Big-Toes to himself. 'I'll stop him coming across the bridge, and tell him he must give me his shopping!'

So next evening there was Big-Toes at the bridge. 'Good evening,' said Tricky, scared.

'Good evening,' said Big-Toes. 'If you want to go across you must give me your bag.'

'Shan't,' said Tricky.

'Then you won't get home tonight,' said Big-Toes, and sat down on the bridge. So, in the end, Tricky had to give him his bag. In it was a currant cake.

'I like cake, but not currants,' said Big-Toes, as he went off with the cake,

Tricky walking behind him, looking miserable.

'Let me take out the currants for you then,' said Tricky at once, and Big-Toes handed it to him. But did Tricky pick out the currants? Not he! He ran off home with the cake, of course!

The next evening Big-Toes was at Rushy Bridge again, waiting for Tricky. 'Give me your shopping!' said Big-Toes, fiercely. 'I'll pay you out for running off with the cake yesterday!'

So Tricky had to hand over his

shopping. In the basket was a pound of butter, a meat-pie and a jam sandwich. Oh, dear, to think of losing all those!

Big-Toes took the basket greedily, and let Tricky cross the bridge. Tricky trotted behind him, ready to cry.

Then he saw that Big-Toes had his beautiful new suit on, and an idea came into his head. He saw a puddle nearby, bent down, filled his hands with water, and threw it all over Big-Toes' head, as he walked along in front.

Big-Toes stopped in alarm. 'My goodness! It's raining! And I've got my best suit on!'

'You'll spoil it,' said Tricky. 'Put up your umbrella quickly, before it gets spotted.'

Big-Toes had his umbrella under his arm. He set down the basket of shopping and began to open his umbrella, which was very stiff. But at last he had it up.

'There,' he said. 'Now I'm all right. Where did I put the basket?'

But, of course, the basket was gone, and Tricky with it! Big-Toes could have danced with rage especially as the sun came out at that minute and he knew that he needn't have stopped to put up his umbrella at all. It was all a trick of Tricky's.

The next evening Big-Toes was again by Rushy Bridge, looking very angry indeed. Tricky had a brown paper parcel, and Big-Toes snatched it from him at once.

'I shall get it back from you!' said Tricky with a laugh. 'I always do. You're so very, very stupid. You don't even think of putting the parcel on the ground and sitting firmly on it till I'm out of sight! That's about the only safe way of keeping a parcel from me.'

'Oho! Is it? Then I'll do that!' said Big-Toes at once. He put the parcel on the ground, and then sat down firmly on it. And no sooner had he sat on it than he leapt up with a squeal of pain.

'Oh! oh! It's pricking me! What's in the parcel?'

'Only my pet hedgehog, who thought he would like to help me to pay you out for your unkindness!' said Tricky, and how he laughed. 'Was he nice to sit on, Big-Toes? He's still stuck to you! All his prickles have come through the paper and he's behind you, sticking fast!'

'Take him off, take him off!' wept Big-Toes, who was a great coward. 'I'll never stop you again, Tricky, never!'

So Tricky pulled off his pet hedgehog, who was enjoying himself very much, and the two set off home together,

163

laughing.

'He won't try and take my shopping again, will he, Prickles?' said Tricky. 'I'll be safe tomorrow when I cross Rushy Bridge.'

So he was. He's a tricky little fellow, isn't he?

15

The Boy who Cheated

Donald was quite a nice boy except when he played games – and then he cheated! Do you know anybody who cheats? They are such a nuisance, aren't they?

Well, Donald cheated when he played cards, and he cheated when he played Ludo or Snakes and Ladders. He'd say he had a six when he hadn't. And he'd say that he'd shouted snap first, when Simon or Tom had – and he'd take up the cards and put them with his pile.

It was really horrid.

'Donald, you're cheating,' his mother would say. 'Donald, don't cheat!' said the children. 'Games are no fun if

somebody cheats!'

But Donald went on cheating, and his mother became very worried, because, you see, if a child cheats when he's little, he'll cheat when he's grown up – and that is very, very bad, and sooner or later there comes a hard punishment.

Still, the other children knew what to do, as you'll soon see.

'Look here, we simply *must* cure Donald!' said Susan.'He's such a nice boy – except at games. But we'll soon hate him if he keeps cheating, because it's so unfair.'

'Yes, but what can we do?' asked Tom. 'We've told him and told him.'

'Telling isn't much good,' said Ronnie. 'We must *show* him what cheating is really like. Now listen! Next time we play games with Donald, we'll *all* cheat – just to show him how horrid it is. He won't like it a bit. Every time we play with him we'll cheat. He'll soon get very tired of it.'

'But I don't want to cheat,' said Susan, who was a very honest and truthful little girl. 'I should feel so horrid and uncomfortable inside if I did. And I should go very red, too.'

'Well, Susan, you won't be *really* cheating,' explained Tom. 'It's just pretend, you know. We'll never, never do it after we've cured Donald. You can be quite sure of that.'

'All right,' said Susan. 'I'll try.'

So that day, after tea, when the four children sat down to play snap, the cheating began. Of course, Donald always did cheat – but the other three

167

cheated too! 'Snap!' cried Ronnie, when there wasn't a snap, and he took up the cards.

'Those two cards weren't alike!' cried Donald angrily. But it was too late. They were in Ronald's pack.

Then, when there was a real snap, Donald shouted snap before the others – he was really first – but Susan calmly took up the cards and put them into *her* pack.

'Susan! You're a cheat! I was first!'

cried Donald in a rage. 'Give me those cards.'

'No, Donald, they're mine,' said Susan and she just wouldn't give them up. Then Tom shouted 'SNAP' and picked up all Donald's cards at once. Donald made a grab at them, but it was too late.

'It wasn't a snap,' he said, almost crying. 'You've taken all my cards. I haven't any left. You're not playing fair.'

'Why, Donald, do you mind that?'

said Susan in surprise. 'You never play fair yourself, do you – so why do you mind us playing the same way as you?'

'I don't want to play cards if you're going to cheat,' said Donald, sulkily. 'Let's play Snakes and Ladders.'

So Ronnie got out the Snakes and Ladders board, and they each chose their counters. You know Snakes and Ladders, don't you? If your counter happens to go on the head of a snake you have to slide down it right to the tail – and if you get at the bottom of a ladder

you may go right up to the top. Of course, it's very nice to get on a ladder, and very horrid to go down a snake.

You can guess that Donald found plenty of ways to cheat at Snakes and Ladders! He *always* counted along the squares so that he came to a ladder and went up it – and he never went down a snake. But this time the others cheated too!

Tom went up the very first ladder he came to. Really, he needed a five to go up, and he had only thrown a four.

171

Donald was very cross. 'You can't go up that ladder,' he said. 'You threw a four. You wanted a five. Go down it again.'

'Certainly not,' said Tom. 'I shall stay at the top.'

Then Susan cheated. She should have gone down a snake, but she didn't, she hopped over its head to the next square. Donald glared at her.

'Susan! You know you should have gone down that snake! Go down at once!'

'No. I'm on the next square,' said Susan.

'Well, you shouldn't be. You should have stopped on that snake's head and gone all the way down,' said Donald.

You know, Donald was so busy scolding the others for cheating that he quite forgot to cheat himself. But when Ronnie cried out that he'd beaten them all, Donald was very angry indeed.

'You haven't won!' he shouted to Ronnie. 'You didn't get the right number to go to the end. You should be *there*,' and he moved Ronnie's counter back-

wards.

'No, I've won, I've won – and you're last!' cried Ronnie.

Donald banged on the board and upset all the counters. They rolled over the floor. 'I shan't play Snakes and Ladders any more with you if you cheat like this!' he cried. 'It isn't any fun.'

'Well, let's play Hide-and-seek,' said Tom, getting up. 'I'll hide my eyes first and count a hundred. Call coo-ee when you're ready.'

Donald loved Hide-and-seek. He was

173

very good at finding splendid places to hide.

'I know a jolly good place,' he said, and he ran off.

'I'm going to peep, Susan and Ronnie,' said Tom. 'Donald is beginning to find that cheating isn't at all pleasant when other people do it – and he won't like it if all his fine hiding-places are found at once.'

So Tom peeped, and he saw that Donald was squeezing himself behind the wood-shed, which was really a very good place to hide indeed.

'You're peeping, you're peeping!' shouted Donald angrily. 'It isn't fair! I shall hide somewhere else!'

Tom counted out loud, 'Seventy-five, seventy-six, seventy-seven, seventy-eight . . .' and he peered to see where Donald was going this time. He saw him running into the raspberry canes.

'A hundred!' shouted Tom. The others all cooeed and Tom ran to find them. He ran straight to the raspberry canes and caught Donald.

'Tom! You cheated! I saw you peeping!' cried Donald. He was beginning to feel very much puzzled at everybody's behaviour. It wasn't like the other children to cheat. Why, they kept winning and he kept losing! This was dreadful! And now Tom had peeped, and he was caught.

'I won't hide *my* eyes,' he said sulkily. 'You peeped and saw where I went.'

'Well, I'll hide *my* eyes then,' said Ronnie, with a grin at the others. So off he went, and began to count a hundred.

He had his hand over his eyes, but he peeped between his fingers to see where Donald went. He saw him dodge behind the greenhouse.

'Coo-ee!' shouted everyone. Ronnie set off to find them, and ran behind the greenhouse at once. He caught Donald, of course, and held him tightly.

'Ronnie, you peeped between your fingers and saw where I went,' said Donald. 'It's no fun playing when people cheat. I shan't play.'

'Well, would you like to play by yourself?' asked Susan, running up. 'We can play without you. And we shan't cheat, either, when we play just by ourselves.'

'I don't want to play by myself,' said Donald, almost in tears. 'I want to play with you. But I don't want you to cheat. Nobody can win or lose properly if you cheat.'

'Do you really think that?' asked Tom. 'Well, Donald, we think that too. A cheat spoils all the fun of the game. But *you* cheat – so we think that whenever

we play with you *we'll* cheat too! Then we'll have a chance of winning. We thought perhaps you'd like us *all* to cheat.'

'Well, I don't,' said Donald, rubbing his eyes hard. 'I hate it. It gives me a nasty sort of feeling. You aren't nice when you cheat.'

'Neither are you,' said Susan. 'In fact, you're horrid, Donald. Well listen – we'll give you a chance. We'll play fair if you will. But if you cheat, we shall! We shall never, never cheat with anybody else, but we think that cheats should be treated differently; so if you start being a cheat again, you'll find that you can only play with cheats – and you won't like that!'

'No, I shan't,' said Donald. 'I won't cheat again. Do believe me! Until you did it to me I didn't really know how horrid it felt. Will you trust me again and play fair? – please, Susan! – please, Tom and Ronnie!'

'Of course we will!' said Susan, and she put her arm round Donald and gave him a squeeze. 'Don't look so worried! We aren't *really* cheats! We just made up this little plan to cure you and to make you nice.'

Well, it did cure Donald. He has never once cheated since. Now he's as honest a child as Susan, and everyone has forgotten that he ever was a cheat. It was a good idea to cure him, wasn't it? It's such a horrid thing to be a cheat. I hope you will never have to play such a trick on any of *your* friends!

16

Belinda's Bicycle

Belinda had a bicycle for her birthday. Mummy thought twice about giving her one because she was so careless with her things. She either broke them or lost them.

'Now, this is a beautiful bicycle, Belinda,' said Mummy. 'You really must take care of it. It has a bell so that you can ring when you go round corners. Keep your bicycle clean and shining, be careful to ring your bell round corners, and don't go into the town on it unless I'm with you.'

'All right, Mummy,' promised Belinda, and she quite meant to keep her word. She cleaned her bicycle twice the first week, always rang the bell to warn anyone she was coming, and didn't get

even a scratch on the paint. Mummy was pleased with her.

'Let me have a ride, Belinda!' begged Harry, who lived next door. 'Do! Just a little one down the garden and back.'

But Belinda wouldn't let him. 'You'd bump into the wall, or fall over, or something,' she said. 'Then you'd spoil my bicycle.'

'I wouldn't. I'm much more careful with my things than you are with yours,' said Harry. 'Who lost her doll in the woods the other week? You! Who

threw her ball up into the tree and couldn't get it? You! Who took her teddy out and left him sitting on a seat in the park, so that he was stolen? You!'

'You're simply horrid,' said Belinda. 'I shan't let you have even a little ride on my bicycle. Go away!'

'You're a mean girl, Belinda,' said Harry. 'I let you play with my new train and I let you help to fly my kite. Keep your nasty old bicycle! I don't want to ride it.'

'Well, you won't,' said Belinda, and

182

she made a horrid face. She could be quite a nasty little girl when her mother wasn't there.

Belinda often went out with her mother, and each time she rode her bicycle. She was very proud of the pretty blue and silver machine, and pedalled along fast. She liked going to the town on it, because it was downhill and the bicycle went very quickly then. Mummy helped to push her back, so that was nice, too.

Mummy called to her one morning: 'Belinda! I've forgotten to fetch your mended shoes and you'll want to wear them this afternoon. Go and fetch them from the cobbler's, will you?'

'Oh! It's such a long way,' grumbled Belinda.

'Nonsense!' said Mummy. 'You've got two strong legs and you'll soon be there. Go along now!'

Belinda went sulkily to get a basket. In the hall was her bicycle. She looked at it. Ah, if she went on that she would soon be there and back.

But Mummy wouldn't let her go to the town on it when she was alone. Bother! Belinda took a quick look round. Mummy was out in the kitchen talking to the plumber. Suppose she got on her bicycle and rode off quickly? Mummy wouldn't know, and she could slip in at the back way when she came home so that nobody would see her.

So Belinda got on her bicycle and rode off quickly. Down the hill she went, very fast, with the pedals flying round and round. To the cobbler's shop she rode and then got off. There were bicycles leaning against the cobbler's window, so Belinda put her bicycle just round the corner by the shop door, in a little passage, out of the way.

She got her mended shoes. When she came out she saw a circus going through the streets, with big vans and cages in a long line – and, good gracious, an elephant! On the vans great letters were painted. Belinda spelt them out.

'Carl Crack's Circus! Oooh! Where's it

going? Look at that baby bear. And, oh, there's a girl with a goose! And are those monkeys?'

Belinda ran down the street after the circus procession. This was fun! Where was the circus going? It was going to camp in the field outside the town. Perhaps Mummy would take her to see it.

Belinda forgot all about her bicycle. She ran along, clutching her mended shoes, and watched the vans turn in at the big field-gate. The elephant helped to pull in one of the biggest vans of all.

Then Belinda suddenly heard the church clock strike one. Goodness! Dinner time. Whatever would Mummy say?

She ran home as fast as she could, panting up the hill. She got in just as dinner was being put on the table.

'What a long time you've been!' said Mummy. 'I was just coming to look for you. Wash your hands and come along, quickly.'

In the middle of her dinner, Belinda

had a most alarming thought. Her bicycle! She had left it somewhere in the town, and come home without it. Where had she left it? Oh, yes, just by the cobbler's.

She went very red as she thought about it. She didn't want to tell Mummy because she would be scolded for going to the town on it by herself. Oh, dear – she must go and fetch it immediately after dinner. How she hoped it would still be there!

She was very ashamed of forgetting about it – her lovely new bicycle, left behind and forgotten! How *could* she do such a thing? Harry was quite right, she was very careless.

After dinner she ran straight down to the town. She looked in the little passage for her bicycle, and her heart went right down into her boots. It wasn't there! The passage was empty.

Tears came into Belinda's eyes. Some body had stolen it! What ought she to do? Go to the police? Go home and tell Mummy? How very, very cross her

mother would be.

Belinda peeped timidly into the cobbler's shop. The cobbler was there, mending shoes. 'Have you seen my bicycle anywhere?' asked Belinda. 'The one I came on this morning? I put it into this passage and now it's gone.'

'Good gracious! It must have been stolen then,' said the cobbler. 'I haven't seen it at all.'

Belinda went home crying. She saw a policeman and wondered if she should tell him, but she was afraid. She had been naughty to disobey her mother, and the policeman might say that it served her right to lose her bicycle.

Mummy wondered why she was crying. Belinda went to her and told her what had happened. The tears ran down the little girl's cheeks, and Mummy looked very serious.

'Oh, Belinda! Your new bicycle! I've told you so often that if we do wrong, something unpleasant always happens. I don't expect you'll ever get that lovely bicycle back. I'll ring up the police.'

The police didn't know anything about the bicycle at all. They promised to look out for it, but they said that if Belinda had been so careless as to leave it in the town for hours, she deserved to lose it.

'Yes, I know I do,' said Belinda, miserably. 'I'm dreadfully sorry, Mummy. My lovely, lovely bicycle! Oh, I do feel so unhappy!'

She went into the garden, crying. Harry put his head over the wall, looking mysterious. 'Belinda! I've got something to tell you. Come here, quick.'

'Where?' asked Belinda.

'Over the wall. Come on,' said Harry. So Belinda climbed over the wall and went with Harry. He took her to the little playshed he had in the garden and opened the door. And *what* do you think was inside?

Yes – Belinda's little blue and silver bicycle! She couldn't believe her eyes. She stared at Harry in the greatest surprise and delight.

'I *thought* you'd be pleased,' said

Harry. 'You were a naughty girl this morning – you left it all by itself and went to look at the circus procession. I saw you. And you forgot to take your bicycle home, because it was still by the cobbler's when I went home. So I brought it back for you.'

'Oh, Harry – you *are* good and kind,' said Belinda, and she gave him a hug. 'But why did you hide it in the shed?'

'Because I thought you would get into dreadful trouble if your mother found out you had left your bicycle down in the town,' said Harry. 'Does she know?'

'Yes, she knows,' said Belinda. 'I would have told her anyhow. I'm awfully sorry I was so silly – and oh, Harry, you *are* nice to have brought my bicycle back when I was so horrid and wouldn't let you ride it.'

She took it out of the shed. 'Get on, Harry,' she said, 'and ride it down the path, round your house, onto the road and into my garden to show Mummy you've got it. She will be so pleased!'

Mummy was very pleased indeed.

'What a kind and sensible little boy you are, Harry,' she said. 'Go and ask your mother if you can come to tea. You and Belinda can play in the garden afterwards.'

Well, Harry came to tea – and I don't know if you can guess what he did afterwards? He rode Belinda's bicycle round and round the garden till his legs couldn't pedal any more!

As for Belinda, she never left her bicycle behind again! She's still got it, and I'm sure she'd let you have a ride on it if you asked her.